NIGHT NIGHT Sleep Tight

THE BODLEY HEAD
LONDON

1 3 5 7 9 10 8 6 4 2

This edition Copyright © The Bodley Head Children's Books

First published in the United Kingdom in 1998
by The Bodley Head Children's Books
Random House, 20 Vauxhall Bridge Road, London SW1V 2SA

Random House Australia (Pty) Limited,
20 Alfred Street, Milsons Point, Sydney
New South Wales 2061, Australia

Random House New Zealand Limited,
18 Poland Road, Glenfield
Auckland 10, New Zealand

Random House South Africa (Pty) Limited,
Endulini, 5A Jubilee Road,
Parktown 2193, South Africa

Random House UK Limited Reg. No. 954009

A CIP catalogue record for this book
is available from the British Library

ISBN 0 370 32308 4

Printed and bound in Singapore

CONTENTS

Frog is Frightened
Max Velthuijs **9**

Dad! I Can't Sleep
Michael Foreman **68**

One Round Moon
and a Star for Me
Ingrid Mennen,
illustrated by Niki Daly **18**

I Want to See the Moon
Louis Baum,
illustrated by Niki Daly **78**

Rabbit Magic
Susie Jenkin-Pearce,
illustrated by Julia Malim **28**

Someone Somewhere
Henrietta Branford,
illustrated by Lesley Harker **87**

Timid Tim and
the Cuggy Thief
John Prater **37**

Why Do Stars Come
Out at Night?
Annalena McAfee,
illustrated by Anthony Lewis **100**

Bedtime
Tony Ross **49**

What is the Moon?
Caroline Dunant,
illustrated by Liz Loveless **105**

Burning the Tree
Shirley Hughes **53**

The Swan
Virginia Mayo **115**

✫ FROG IS FRIGHTENED

Max Velthuijs

Frog was very frightened. He was lying in bed, and
he could hear strange noises everywhere. There was
a creaking in the cupboard and a rustling under the
floorboards.
"Somebody is under my bed," thought Frog.
He jumped out of bed and ran through the dark
woods until he reached Duck's house.
"How nice of you to come and see me," said Duck.
"But it is rather late. I'm about to go to bed."

☾ 9

"Please, Duck," said Frog. "I'm frightened. There's a ghost under my bed."

"Nonsense," laughed Duck. "There's no such thing."

"There is," said Frog. "The woods are haunted as well."

"Don't be frightened," said Duck. "You can stay with me. I'm not afraid."

And they huddled into bed together. Frog cuddled
Duck's warm body and wasn't frightened any more.
All of a sudden they heard a scratching noise on the
roof.
"What was that?" asked Duck, sitting up with a jolt.
The next moment they heard a creaking on the stairs.
"This house is haunted too!" shouted Frog. "Let's get
out of here."
And they ran out into the woods. Frog and Duck ran
as fast as they could. They felt there were ghosts and
scary monsters everywhere.

Eventually they reached Pig's house and, gasping for breath, they hammered on the door.

"Who is it?" asked a sleepy voice.

"Please, Pig, open the door. It's us," shouted Frog and Duck.

"What's the matter?" asked Pig angrily. "Why have you woken me up in the middle of the night?"

"Please help us," said Duck. "We're terrified. The woods are full of ghosts and monsters."

Pig laughed. "What nonsense. Ghosts and monsters don't exist. You know that."

"Well, look for yourself," said Frog.

Pig looked out of the window, but he couldn't see anything unusual.

"Please, Pig, may we sleep here? We're so scared."

"OK," said Pig. "My bed is big enough. And I am never frightened. I don't believe in all that rubbish."

So there they were, all three of
them together in Pig's bed.
"This is nice," thought Frog.
"Nothing can happen now."
But they couldn't sleep. They
listened to all the strange,
frightening noises in the woods.
This time, Pig heard them too!
But luckily the three friends
could comfort each other. They
shouted out that they were not
scared – that they weren't afraid
of anything. Eventually they fell
asleep, exhausted.

Next morning, Hare went to visit
Frog. The door was wide open and
Frog was nowhere to be seen.
"This is strange," thought Hare.
Duck's house was also empty.
"Duck, Duck, where are you?"
shouted Hare. But there was no
answer. Hare was very worried.
He thought something terrible
must have happened.
Terrified, he ran through the
woods looking for Frog and Duck.
He looked and looked but there
was no trace of his friends.

"Perhaps Pig will know where they are," he thought.
Hare knocked on Pig's door. There was no answer.
It was very quiet. He looked in through the window
and there he saw his three friends lying in bed, fast
asleep. It was ten o'clock in the morning! Hare
knocked on the window.
"Help! A ghost!" shouted the three friends.
Then they saw that it was Hare.

Pig unlocked the door and they all ran outside.
"Oh, Hare," they said. "We were so frightened.
The wood is full of ghosts and scary monsters."
"Ghosts and monsters?" said Hare, surprised.
"They don't exist."
"How do you know?" said Frog angrily. "There
was one under my bed."
"Did you see it?" asked Hare quietly.
"Well, no," said Frog. He hadn't *seen* it but he
had heard it.
They talked about ghosts and monsters and other
ghastly things for a long time.

Pig made some breakfast.
"You know," said Hare. "Everyone is frightened sometimes."
"Even you?" asked Frog, surprised.
"Oh yes," said Hare. "I was very frightened this morning when I thought you were lost."

16

There was a silence.
Then everyone laughed.
"Don't be ridiculous, Hare," said Frog.
"You have nothing to fear. We are always here."

ONE ROUND MOON AND A STAR FOR ME

Ingrid Mennen and Niki Daly

One round moon.
So many stars.
A falling star, Mama!
Look how Papa catches it in his warm
brown blanket.
See how it slips into his silver milk bucket.
"A star for a new baby," says Mama.
Now, Moon, please go! Go to your home.
Go to sleep in your hut. Roll up night.

Look how Sun is chasing
Moon, Mama.
Big round moon, back to her
empty hut.
Ah! There! One round sun!
Hurry through the grass – make
it gold. Run over the hill, past
Papa's herd.
Come, Sun, here!
Come warm our home.
For there's a brand new baby in
our hut today.

Makazi - my aunty - lifts me high. I stick two stalks of sun-yellow grass in the roof, above the door.

Makazi says, "Now the men will come in only when the inkaba-cord falls from the baby's belly." Nomsa, Sindi and Nono bring water for the baby, balancing buckets on their heads.

Sis Beauty brings a new cake of soap she has saved for so long. Sis Anna brings a little paraffin lamp made from a tin and a piece of wick-cloth to light for the baby. Gogo - our grandmother - and her friends bring fresh cow-dung for a new floor. Inside, Mama sings a tula-tula hush-hush song to the baby. And then Papa comes. He leaves his silver bucket, brimming with milk, at the door and kneels to look at the baby's two tiny hands.

"They look like my hands," he says.

He looks at the baby's tiny round ears. "Mama's ears."

He unwraps the blanket, and there are two small feet with ten tiny toes.

"They will walk well." Papa nods.

"I'm the baby's father," says Papa with a smile.

We walk to the other men, but my heart feels dark, like a night with no moon.

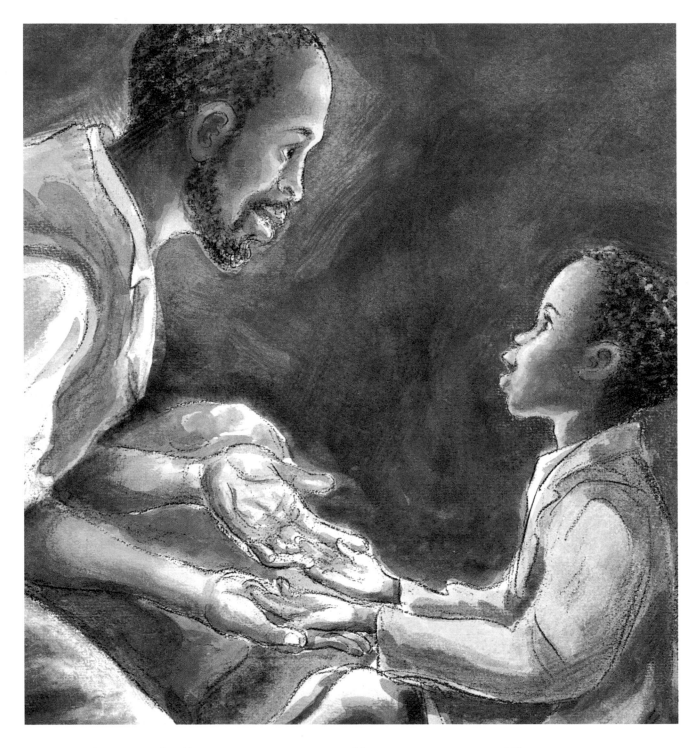

At last I ask, "Papa, are you really my papa too?"
He takes my hands and puts them next to his. "See," he says.
"I am really your papa too."
He looks me close in the eye. "Your eyes are like Mama's eyes.
You are your papa's child and you are your mama's child."

He puts his arms around me and says, "Tonight, when the
moon is big and round and the stars light up God's great sky,
I'll show you, there is also a star for you."

One round moon.
And a star for me.

RABBIT MAGIC

*Susie Jenkin-Pearce
and Julia Malim*

November grey, end of day.
Mist time,
 smoke time,
  rabbit time,

   magic time.

Small boy follows through the
gate. Golden time, berry time,
crimson leaves in the lake.
Footsteps follow, join the chase.
Where to? Where next?
Look around.
What's hiding there in autumn
leaves and evening light?

The moon shines down
as secret friends dance
on into the night.

Follow rabbit through his door,
time is passing into sleep.
Falling snow, winter time,
peaceful snow, feather soft.

Spring sun shines and small
boy wakes, follow rabbit,
flutter wings.
Buds unfurl and thrush sings
sweet, the season's green, the
blossom's pink.

Small boy follows through
the arch, to gold and blue.
The spring has passed.
Silent heat and poppy red,
a summer's beauty will not last.

Danger, rabbit! Race through seasons.
Follow small boy back to safety,

back to mist and bonfire burning,
frosty air and warm soft bed.

November grey, end of day.
Mist time, smoke time, rabbit time,

magic time.

TIMID TIM AND THE CUGGY THIEF

John Prater

Tim was a shy little boy.
He wasn't very brave, and didn't like noisy,
messy fun or being splashed or rough
and tumbles. He didn't like big adventures.

He only wanted to be still and quiet, with his special soft and sleepy blanket, his cuggy. He took his cuggy everywhere, and kept it close by him always. The other children would sometimes tease him by singing the CUGGY THIEF SONG!

Look out! Beware the cuggy thief
Who creeps around at night,
And steals away your favourite things
If you don't hug them tight!
They say he can be frightened off
If you put up a fight!
But none of us would ever dare
Face such an awful sight.

One dark and windy night, Tim lay in bed, holding his cuggy tight. But when he fell asleep, he tossed and turned – and let it go!

A chilling blast of air blew through the bedroom, and Tim awoke to find his cuggy gone. He let out a little cry, which grew bigger, and bigger, and bigger... until he yelled at the top of his voice, "Come back, you thief! You rascal! Give me back my cuggy!"

Tim leapt out into the night to catch the thief.

The streets were dark and empty.

The wood was darker still.

The path was steep, the mud was deep, and though his heart beat fast,

Tim never took his eyes off the wicked rogue ahead.

The weather grew wild, and the waves crashed loud.

But Tim bravely kept going on. He knew that he was getting close to the cuggy thief's dreadful lair.
He took a deep breath, then boldly entered the dim and rocky hole.
"Give me back my cuggy," he yelled.

Tim grabbed his cuggy.

"It's mine," he shouted.

The startled cuggy thief grew bigger, and bigger, and bigger, let out a horrid scream, and turned to pounce...

But Tim did not run. He stood quite still, and faced that awful sight.

The horrid scream grew faint until it was no more than the distant whistling of the wind. His huge darkness grew pale and thin, until it was no more than the smoke curling from the fire.

"Phew!" said Tim. "Serves you right." He knew there was nothing left of that horrid villain. The cuggy thief was gone for ever.

Tim gathered together all the cuggies, teddies and best-loved toys in the wicked robber's hoard.

The boat was full for the journey home.

Everyone cheered the hero Tim
for being the bravest boy ever.

But even the bravest boy ever still cuddled cuggy
for just a little longer.

BEDTIME
Tony Ross

Time for your bath.

But I'm not dirty yet.

That's

better.

Time for your bath.

I'd rather wash my hands.

I'd rather wash my face.

I'd rather clean my teeth.

I'd rather brush my hair.

Oooh! I don't want a bath.

I'd rather go to bed.

Why?

There's a spider in the bath

... and Ted's in bed.

BURNING THE TREE
Shirley Hughes

William and Grandpa were taking down the tree. Christmas was over and it was time to put all the decorations away in the loft until next year. Grandpa pulled off the shiny glass balls and handed them to William who laid them carefully in their box. They took down the tinsel and unwound the fairy lights.

Then they wrapped the two little glass birds and the angel with golden wings in tissue paper and put them away too.

When they had finished, the tree looked rather bald and old without its sparkle. The presents which had been stacked underneath its boughs had all been opened on Christmas day, of course. And it no longer smelt of that wonderful foresty green smell as it had when they bought it. It leaned sideways in its pot. A lot of needles came off and scattered on the carpet.

"What a mess!" said Mum. "I'll never get them all up. You'd better move it out of the way, you two." And she briskly plugged in the vacuum cleaner. Vacuuming always put her in a bossy mood.

William and Grandpa laid the Christmas tree in a dust sheet and dragged it as far as the back door, trying not to leave a trail of pine needles behind them.

"Get your coat. We'll have a bonfire," said Grandpa.

William found his coat. Then he followed Grandpa to the door of his room and waited while he looked for his old gardening jacket.

Grandpa had not lived at William's house for very long, only since Gran had died. He had his own room and his own television set. It was quite a small room and it was very full of things.

There were some photographs on the mantel shelf, one of Gran and Grandpa on their wedding day, one of Mum when she was a baby and one of Grandpa's football team. Grandpa was right in the middle, holding the ball, because he was the goalkeeper.

William spent a lot of time in Grandpa's room. Sometimes they watched television and sometimes they just chatted. William loved hearing about all the adventures Grandpa had had when he was a young man, and looking at his things. There was one special box, a polished wooden one with brass handles, which stood on the high shelf above the books. Grandpa never showed anyone what was in there.

But William had seen inside the box. He had peeped into it one day when Grandpa was out. He just couldn't resist the temptation.

It was a sad disappointment. There was nothing interesting to see, only some boring old letters, a train ticket, a few pressed flowers and some papers which looked like poems but the writing was too difficult for William to read. Afterwards William felt miserable and uncomfortable when he looked at the box. He felt bad about knowing what was in there when Grandpa didn't know he knew. He tried hard to forget all about it.

It was nearly dark when they went outside, with only a streak of red left in the sky. William and Grandpa dragged the tree down to the rubbish heap at the bottom of the garden. It was Grandpa's special place behind the greenhouse by the end wall. He spent a lot of time there, piling up leaves and garden rubbish. Then he would lean on his rake and light his pipe. Mum didn't like Grandpa to smoke indoors. She said she couldn't stand the smell.

They heaved the tree on to the big pile of leaves and twigs which was already there. Its bare arms stuck up bravely into the sky.

Grandpa went indoors again and fetched out a big bag full of old paper chains and dry holly which had decorated the hall. He packed them round the tree. Then he pulled out his matches and set light to them.

"This will make a grand blaze," he told William. The paper and holly caught at once and burned brightly. Then they flared into white ash and the twigs and leaves started to smoulder and crackle and give off smoke. Flames began to lick through them, small at first, creeping up towards the tree. When they reached the dry pine needles the whole thing suddenly took fire.

Flames shot up with great eddies of smoke. The Christmas tree branches were all at once bright and glowing, covered with festive sparks. As William watched, the wall behind him seemed to melt and quiver. His eyes were watering, but the smell was wonderful. They stood and looked at the fire for a long time. They watched until at last the tree burned out and collapsed into the pits and caves of ash.

Then Mum called William indoors. He left Grandpa standing there, staring into the fire.

Later, when it was quite dark, Grandpa was still out there. They could see the red glow at the bottom of the garden.

"Supper will be ready in ten minutes," said Mum, as she drew the curtains. "Run and tell him, will you, William?"

William put on his coat again and ran down the garden path. Grandpa was standing exactly where he had left him. But he had something under his arm. It was the box with brass handles.

"Let's have one more good blaze before bedtime," said Grandpa as William joined him. And then he opened the box and flung all the letters and things that were inside on to the bonfire. Just like that! They caught alight instantly, and once again the cheerful flames leapt up.

"But I thought they were special," said William as they watched them burn.

"They were," said Grandpa, "but it's not things that are important really. The special things are in my head. And my heart. So why not get rid of the rest?"

William had never heard Grandpa say anything like that before. He didn't quite know how to answer. He took Grandpa's hand and stood leaning up against him until the flames died down and were finally gone.

"I looked into your box once," said William.

"That's all right. You were welcome," said Grandpa. "They made a grand blaze, didn't they?" he added, after a pause.

William suddenly felt happy. "Mum says I can stay up a bit and watch the football on television, as it's Saturday," he told Grandpa. "Will you watch it with me?"

"You bet I will!" said Grandpa. "You run along and tell Mum I'll be in just as soon as I've finished this pipe."

☆ DAD! I CAN'T SLEEP ☆
Michael Foreman

Little Panda couldn't sleep.
"Mum!" he called. "Can I have a drink?"
Mum said, "It's your turn, Dad. I've done enough today."
Dad took Little Panda a drink, kissed him goodnight and
went downstairs.
"Dad!" called Little Panda. "I still can't sleep. Can I have
another drink?"

"No," said Dad. "Go to sleep."

"I can't," said Little Panda.

"Count sheep," said Dad. "Then you'll go to sleep."

"How?" said Little Panda.

Dad climbed the stairs and sat on Little Panda's bed.

"How do I count sheep, Dad?" asked Little Panda.

"Just close your eyes," said Dad. "Now imagine sheep jumping over a fence. Count them as they jump. One. Two. Three. Four. Five. Six. Then you will fall asleep."

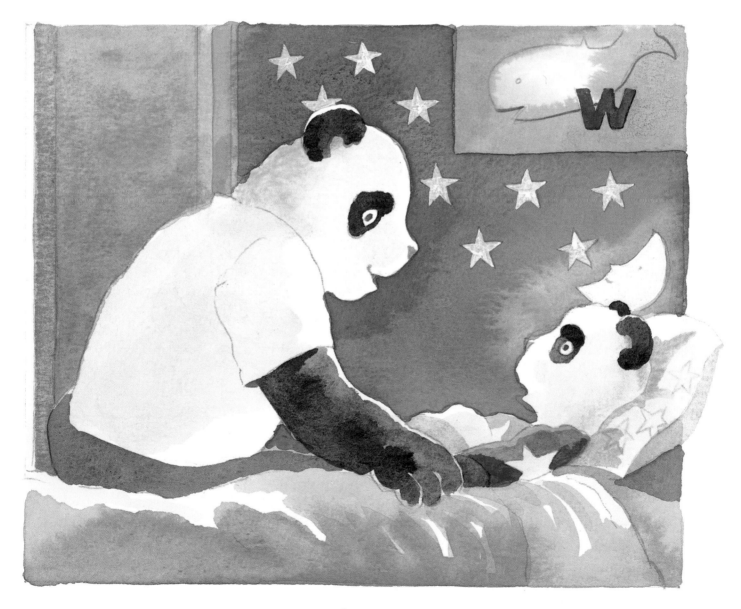

Little Panda closed his eyes
and counted sheep.
"One. Two. Three. Four. Five
and a lamb. Six. Seven and
another lamb..."
Quietly, Dad went downstairs.

"Dad!" called Little Panda.
"I can't sleep."
"Count sheep!" called Dad.
"I've done that and I still can't sleep," called Little Panda.
"Count something else," shouted Dad. "Count cows!"
Little Panda closed his eyes and counted cows.
"One. Two. Three. Four. Five. Six. Seven. Eight. Nine. Dad! I still can't sleep."

"I am not coming up again!" shouted Dad. "Count pigs or tigers!"
Little Panda counted tigers.
"Sixteen. Seventeen. Eighteen. Nineteen tigers and three little pigs. Dad! I still can't sleep."
"Count elephants! And I don't want to hear from you again," shouted Dad.
Little Panda counted elephants.
"Forty-six. Forty-seven. Forty-eight. Forty-nine."

Then he counted rhinos and hippos, giraffes and polar bears, and still he couldn't sleep.

"Dad! I've counted all sorts of things and I still can't sleep."

"Dinosaurs!" shouted Dad. "Have you counted dinosaurs?"

"No," said Little Panda.

"Well, count dinosaurs. And you know there are lots of different kinds. Make sure you count all of them. AND GO TO SLEEP!"

Little Panda started to count dinosaurs.

"Two hundred and two diplodocuses. Two hundred and three diplodocuses. Two hundred and four diplodocuses. Forty-six stegosauruses. Forty-seven stegosauruses..."

But still Little Panda couldn't sleep.
"Two zillion pterodactyls. Two zillion and one
pterodactyls. Two zillion and... Dad! Dad!"
"What is it now?" yelled Dad, as
he threw the laundry at the cat
and stomped up the stairs.
He pushed open Little
Panda's door.

"Dad," said Little Panda.
"We all want a·drink."

I WANT TO SEE THE MOON

Louis Baum and Niki Daly

Toby woke up in the middle of the night.

"Daddy," he called, "Daddy."

Toby listened as Daddy's footsteps came up the stairs.

"Hello, Toby!" said Daddy, as he lifted Toby in his arms.

"I want to see the moon," said Toby.

"Would you like to make a wee first?" asked Daddy.

"Yes," said Toby.

They went to the bathroom.

"I want to see the moon," said Toby.

"Now let's put on a clean nappy," said Daddy.
"I want to see the moon," said Toby.
Daddy filled a glass of water for Toby.
"I want to see the moon," said Toby.
"Let's go downstairs for a little while," said Daddy.
"I'll give you a piggyback."
"I want to see the moon," said Toby.

In front of the fire was Toby's favourite book, still
open where he had left it.
"Let's read a story," said Daddy.
"I want to see the moon," said Toby.
Under the kitchen table were Toby's building bricks,
just where he had left them.
"Let's build a castle," said Daddy, "a big castle with
chimneys and windows and turrets and things."
"I want to see the moon," said Toby.

"Do you know what I've got for you?" said Daddy.
"A lovely mug of warm milk."
"I don't want a lovely mug of warm milk," said Toby.
"I know what you want," said Daddy, "you want to
see the moon."
"Yes, please, I want to see the moon," said Toby.
So they went outside, into the garden, to look at
the moon...

But the moon wasn't there.
There was nothing in the sky but big black clouds.
But a little wind was blowing.
It was blowing the big black clouds across the sky.
Every now and then a little light from the moon shone through.
The moon was playing hide-and-seek behind the clouds.

"Where's the moon, Daddy?" asked Toby.

"Ssh," said Daddy. "If we wait here a little while and watch very closely, the wind will blow the clouds across the sky until the moon breaks through the clouds and –"

"There's the moon!" said Toby.
"It's a beautiful moon," said Daddy.
"Beautiful moon," said Toby.

"Goodnight, moon," said Toby.

SOMEONE SOMEWHERE

Henrietta Branford and Lesley Harker

There was once a child who never knew her mother. Well, perhaps she did when she was very little. But time passed, she did not see her any more, and slowly she forgot her.

She was brought up by a nurse who made her wash her hands and brush her hair and eat cabbage and change her socks and go to bed at bedtime.

The nurse taught her everything she needed to know, especially all the things she must never do. "Promise me," she said, "NEVER to play in the deep, dark forest."

"Why not?" asked the child.

"Because nobody knows what's in there," said the nurse. And that, she thought, was that.

But it wasn't.

Time passed and the child forgot her mother's face, her voice, the smell of her skin, and how she used to sing at night. And the more she forgot her, the more she missed her, until one day she could bear it no longer.

The child remembered her nurse's warning: nobody knows what's in the forest.

But then, she thought, nobody knows what isn't. Maybe all that I have lost is in there.

And off she went to find out.

She came to the edge of the town and there beyond lay the deep, dark forest. And in she went, and on she went, and the trees grew thick about her, and she began to feel afraid.

Wouldn't you?

"Hello?" called the child. "Is anybody there?"

Nobody seemed to be, and she walked on.

Presently she met an old woman.

"What are you doing alone in the forest?" asked the old woman.

"Looking for something," said the child.

"What are you looking for?" asked the old woman.

The child shook her head. She couldn't remember what she was looking for. She only knew that it was something nice, and she wanted it.

"Never mind," said the old woman. "I want a child to fetch my firewood and trim my toenails and catch my cat and dish up my dinner. You'll do."

"No I won't!" said the child, and she ran off under the treees.

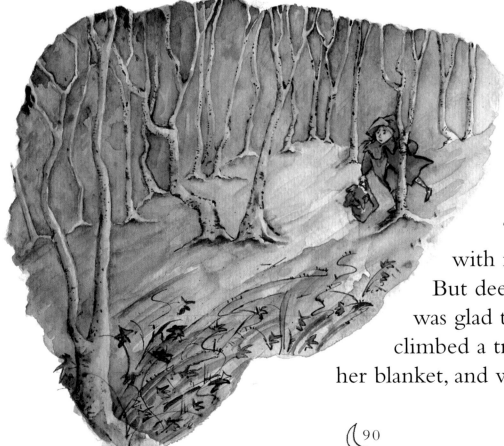

Night began to fall, creepy and spooky, the way it does in the forest, and the child began to think about witches and wolves.

"I wish I had stayed with my nurse," she said. But deep in her heart she was glad that she hadn't. So she climbed a tree, wrapped herself in her blanket, and went to sleep.

In the morning things looked better, and she went on her way.

She came to a little hut in a clearing and outside on a rickety bench there sat a woodman.

"What are you doing in the forest?" asked the woodman.

"Looking for something," said the child.

"What are you looking for?" asked the woodman.

The child shook her head. She couldn't remember what she was looking for. She knew only that it was something nice, and she wanted it.

"Don't go," said the woodman. "Stay here with me."

"No!" said the child. "I would rather be lonely on my own until I find what I am looking for."

On she went, until she came to a dark river winding through the forest. The river turned around a pile of rocks and spread itself into a deep, still pool.

A boat bobbed on the water and a woman waved at her. "Come over," she called. "Come to lunch!"

"Thank you, I will," called the child, and she climbed into a rowing boat.

"We're sailing on down river after lunch," the woman said. "Will you give up your search and come with us?"

"No," said the child, "I cannot."

Night fell, and with it fell the first snow of winter.

Snow's early, thought the child. I must find shelter for tonight.

She looked around, and off in the distance she saw a most peculiar sight. A big old hollow log lay on its side, half buried in glistening snow. From out of each end of the hollow log blew plumes of steam. As she grew nearer to the log the child heard a deep rumbling grumble which came and went with the plumes of steam.

"Thank goodness I brought my torch," she said to herself, and she bent down and shone a beam of yellow light into the hollow log. Inside the log the child saw one of the most comfortable and comforting sights she had ever seen.

There was a mother bear, and a father bear, and three cubs, all curled and cuddled and cossetted around each other in a great furry heap of steam-breathing, rumble-grumbling, sleepy-winter-hibernation-bearfulness.

"Mother!" she whispered. "I've found you! Can I come in?"

Deep in her winter sleep, the mother bear heard the child. "Of course you can," she growled.

So the child crawled into the hollow log and settled herself comfortably against the big velvet stomach of the mother bear, and there she stayed all winter.

Spring came to the forest around April. Suddenly the winter was past, flowers appeared and the birds sang from dawn till dusk.

The bears stretched, and breathed deep, and scratched six months' worth of itches.

The cubs looked out of the hollow log at the greening forest. They heard birds singing and bees buzzing and they scrambled to their feet and set off to explore the woods.

Father Bear looked at Mother Bear. "How about a walk in the woods?" he said.

Just then Mother Bear caught sight of the child, still asleep in the log.

"Wait a minute," she said. "There's a child in our log. I remember now. She came in last October when the snow was falling. She called me Mother."

"She looks like breakfast to me," said Father Bear.

"Don't be so unkind," scolded Mother Bear. "I'm going to wake her up."

So Father Bear went off on his own feeling grumpy, and Mother Bear gently woke the sleeping child.

"Good morning, poppet," she said, licking the child with her warm wet tongue. "Did you sleep well?"

"Yes thank you, Mother," said the child. "Once I found you I slept like a log."

"In a log," corrected Mother Bear gently. "You slept *in* a log. And now it is spring. My cubs have gone off into the wide world to seek their fortunes, and I suppose you'll be wanting to do the same."

"Will I?" asked the child.

"I expect so," said Mother Bear, with a sigh.

The child looked at herself. She had grown, but not as much as the young bears. She had found a mother. She had slept through the spring and through the bitter winter, safe on her mother's belly.

"If it's all the same to you, Mother," she said, "I will stay with you through the spring, and through the summer and the autumn too. I will sleep one more winter with you in the hollow log. After that, I may go off to seek my fortune. I'll see how I feel."

Mother Bear smiled a warm wide smile. "It's better than all the same to me, my child," she answered.

"Then I'll stay," said the child. And she did.

Wouldn't you?

WHY DO STARS COME OUT AT NIGHT?

Annalena McAfee and Anthony Lewis

Why do stars come out
at night?
Because the moon is scared
of the dark.

leep?

Because our dreams must go out to play.

WHAT IS THE MOON?
Caroline Dunant and Liz Loveless

What is the moon?
It's a light in the sky that makes
the dark bright.

Does it shine every night?
Sometimes we can't see it
but the moon is still there.

But where is it, where?
It might go behind clouds,
maybe to sleep,
or to play
hide and seek.

Will it play with me?
We'll see, but now
it's time for your tea.
Why is the moon so high?
What's it doing up there?
At the top of the world,
like the top of a tree,
the moon hangs by a ribbon
that no one can see.

What colour is it?
Why doesn't it show?
And how do you know?
I was told it is black, a long time ago.

Can I fly up and see?
Not just now. It's time for your tea.

Is the moon very old?
Is it hot, is it cold?

The moon changes shape,
but it has always been there.
You would need a coat,
or something warm to wear.

What shapes do you mean?
Can you please show me?
I will, and then it's
time for your tea.
Now, hold up your hands
and we will try
to make shapes of the moon
changing in the sky.

Into the curve of the right,
fits the moon when it's new.

Make a circle with both
and the full moon's in view.

Then curve to the left,
to fit the moon when it's old.
And that is what I was always told.

Can you do that again?
Can I try?
Can I see how the moon fits together with my hands and me?
Just once more, then you must have your tea.

But there's still so much that I don't know.
Is the moon made of snow?
There are mountains and valleys and wide open spaces.

It looks too small to have so many places.

The moon is a world as big as ours but no people are there, it just lives with the stars.

That sounds very sad. I'll fly up and see
if the moon would like to play with me.
No, not right now, it's so far away,
to get there would take a year and a day.

But look at the sky, the moon is so near.
It seems that way, because the night is clear.

But Mum, can't you see, it's waving to me...
I'm going right now to the moon for my tea.

THE SWAN
Virginia Mayo

One day Mum and Rob and I went to the country.
We had a picnic. Mum said if we were lucky we might see
some ducks or geese. We were very lucky. We saw a *swan*.

He swam very close to me. "Hello," I said.
Mum told me that swans fall in love and stay together
all their lives. If they are parted, the one left behind is
so sad that it pines away and dies.

Then I noticed a fisherman and his little boy. Their line broke and the fisherman threw it back in the water.

Mum was angry. She said the swans could get tangled in his line and the lead weights could poison them. I thought perhaps the man didn't know that he might hurt the swans, so I told him. "Mind your own business!" he said.

Back at home I told Mum that I didn't understand how anyone could hurt animals.

I thought about my swan and how he had looked at me as if I was his friend.

That night I had a dream. Someone tapped at my window.

When I woke up, for a moment I didn't know where I was.
Then I remembered my dream.
Mum came in to get me dressed. "Look," she said. "A swan's
feather. It must have caught on your clothes."

123

Later that summer we went back to the river.
We took a picnic. Mum said if we were lucky we might see some swans. We were *very* lucky. We saw a mum and a dad and six babies!
"Swans fall in love and stay together all their lives," I told Rob. They swam up close to show me their babies... and they looked right at me as if they knew I was their friend.

Acknowledgements

THE PUBLISHERS GRATEFULLY ACKNOWLEDGE PERMISSION TO REPRODUCE THE
FOLLOWING STORIES, WHICH ARE PUBLISHED IN LONGER, COMPLETE EDITIONS
UNDER THEIR OWN IMPRINTS:

Frog is Frightened, © 1994 by Max Velthuijs,
reprinted by permission of Lothrop, Lee & Shepard Books, and Andersen Press

From One Round Moon and a Star For Me by Ingrid Mennen, illustrated by Niki Daly.
Text copyright © 1994 by Ingrid Mennen. Illustrations copyright © 1994 by Niki Daly.
Reprinted by permission of Orchard Books, New York.

Rabbit Magic, published by The Bodley Head,
text © 1993 by Susie Jenkin-Pearce, illustrations © 1993 by Julia Malim

Timid Tim and the Cuggy Thief, published by The Bodley Head,
© 1993 by John Prater

Bedtime: Little Princess Board Books, copyright © 1995 by Tony Ross,
reprinted by permission of Harcourt Brace & Company, and Andersen Press

Burning the Tree, from *Stories by Firelight*, © 1993 by Shirley Hughes,
reprinted by permission of Lothrop, Lee & Shepard Books

Dad! I Can't Sleep, © 1994 by Michael Foreman,
reprinted by permission of Andersen Press

I Want to See the Moon, published by The Bodley Head,
text © 1984 by Louis Baum, illustrations © 1984 by Niki Daly

Someone Somewhere, published by The Bodley Head,
text © 1995 by Henrietta Branford, illustrations © 1995 by Lesley Harker

Why Do Stars Come Out at Night? (an extract), published by Julia MacRae Books,
text © 1997 by Annalena McAfee, illustrations © 1997 by Anthony Lewis

What is the Moon? published by The Bodley Head,
text © 1993 by Caroline Dunant, illustrations © 1993 by Liz Loveless

The Swan, published by The Bodley Head,
© 1993 by Virgina Mayo